# I am what God says that I am

*Written By*
*R.J. Davis*

*I Am What God Says I Am!*

*ISBN 978-1-940831-64-0*

*Published by Mocy Publishing, LLC.*

*Website: www.mocypublishing.com*

*Email: info@mocypublishing.com*

# I am who God says that I am!

1 Corinthians 15: 10 .... But by the grace of God I am what I am: and his grace which was bestowed upon me was not in vain; but I labored more abundantly than they all; yet not I, but the grace of God which was with me. KJV

# I have the Power to BECOME!

*Love yourself first so that you can welcome the change that's about to happen. Love is the Master key. 1Cor 13:4-7*

*R.J.Davis*

*By: R.J.Davis*

*JeaMaea Divine Inspirations*

# *Introductory*

*Many of us struggle with insecurities throughout our lifetime.*

*Whether it's how we look physically (not being pretty enough), Mentally not knowing how to handle the pressures of life nor knowing how smart you really are. Then spiritually feeling that God has forgotten all about you. But in reality, these very things that you are struggling with are building your character and growing you to be the best version of self. Just know that God created us in his own image and likeness. God's love is everlasting through and through just trust and faith in the process.*

Once you start to feel good about yourself it's like a gateway that opens which gives you a different perspective on life. It gives you a boost of Confidence within yourself. Because no one is perfect we all are human. But to know that you are still beautiful in your brokenness and accepting the person of which you are is Power. When you find the courage and strength to fight through the struggle is where you begin to reclaim the love and power for yourself. You will start to feel empowered, uplifted, motivated and inspired through this journey of creating a world full of encouragement through these affirmations. Learning the value in self-love, self-care will implode over to yourself worth, because you are important.

Healing from the past hurts so that you can live a life that you create for yourself through your words. You will learn to embrace your flaws and imperfections to love who you are. This would then create a foundation that you can build on starting with self and learning to be humbled through the experiences of life.

Scripture say's in Jude 1:20 & 21

But you, Beloved, building up yourselves on your most holy faith, praying in the Holy Spirit. Keep yourselves in the love of God, looking for the mercy of our Lord Jesus Christ unto eternal life. (KJV)

Then you can welcome all the joy that life will bring.

Respecting yourself and loving yourself will make you feel whole.

# Description

Affirmations are ways to help encourage or build yourself up. It gives a sense of knowing that you have purpose. It helps to transform your mindset and declare a new belief about yourself. The power of your words that you speak over your life motivates us to become better than who we were each day. By renewing your mind, it assists you to access something greater and allows you to achieve your goals in life by changing the narrative from a negative to a positive. Believing is achieving and evident of this hoped for so that the words we speak will start to take root.

Scripture says in Romans 12:2 And be not conformed to this world: but be ye transformed by the renewing of your mind, that ye may prove what is that good and acceptable, and perfect will of God. KJV Understand everything that is spoken over your life will come to pass. The power of your word is the *manifestation of what you want your life to look like. Therefore, learn to speak life into every aspect of your life and watch it transform to something great.*

*Proverbs 18:21 reads, Death and life are in the power of the tongue and they that love it shall eat the fruit thereof.*

## Benefits

The benefit of having a renewed mindset creates a pathway for more growth, more potential and it strengthens you as a person. The power of one's mindset governs the way we face life challenges, and it molds and shapes you into the person of which you are. In the words of Muhammed Ali "Champions **aren't made in the gyms. Champions are made from something deep inside them: a desire, a dream, a vision. They must have last minute stamina. They must be a little faster. They must have the skills and the will, but the will must be stronger than the skill".**

Therefore, by knowing that your words have power it bares fruit of God's promise to live in a land flowing with milk and honey. *Exodus 3:8 (KJV)*

So, put your word into action and live the life that you speak. To do this, start with a little prayer/ meditation and ask God to guide and strengthen you on this journey to speak positively of your life.

## Let your Heart be filled with Praise

**Example 1:** Lord, I humbly come to you this day whole heartedly and trusting you because you know all that I am.

**Example 2:** Lord, as I pray or say these affirmations over my life that you will align my heart to take root into the words that I declare over my life, may it be released in the atmosphere so be it.

**Example 3:** I Am now living in my Highest timeline, Every day, I'm met with blessings and abundance.

However, you want to start your day out and always include God to help you along the way.

Thus, in the morning before you leave to start the day it is important to set the tone of what kind of day you want to have so start it by having Gratitude and an Affirmation.

**Just for Today I will learn to breathe and be thankful for my many Blessings.**

## Daily Challenge

*In doing so, start by choosing an affirmation that you can stand on for the week or even for that month. Begin by saying the affirmation of your choice daily and even write it down on a sticky note and put it somewhere you can see it so that you can say it. Over the course of the next few days try to pay attention to your emotions, your behavior, the atmosphere around you, even the kind of people you attract. So that you can witness the growth and the subtle changes. For instance, your thought process should start focusing on more positive things. This is how you will know that your mindset has shifted for better.*

**When I Rise, I Choose to Be.......**
**Start Each day with a Grateful Heart!**

*Create your own affirmations. Ask yourself… How did it make you feel? Physically, Emotionally, Spiritually, and Mentally. What did you learn about yourself?)*

# Poem

*I inhale positive energy and exhale any fears. I will not worry about things that are out of my control. I am no longer afraid of what could go wrong. I focus on what is going right. I will calmly think of solutions to any problems that may arise. I can handle anything that comes my way. - Magen Harper Nicholes (MHN)*

*I am Undergoing a powerful transformation; I enable my best self by maintaining a positive attitude*

*I walk in the Boldness of Christ*

*God's will be my reality*

*I Am a power warrior anointed with his oil*

*I Love myself just as I Am*

*I Rise above all measures*

*I Speak life into every are of my life*

*I Choose to evolve into someone Greater awaken the gifts inside of me*

*I Reside in the Land of Goshen*

*I'm stepping into my higher self*

*My Confidence and Positive attitude exude me*

*Start each day with a Grateful Heart*

*My Light illuminates my path of Clarity and Abundance*

*I Am planted on Fertile Ground*

*My soil is fruitful*

*God's Strength is my Strength*

*I Am Clothed with Confidence*

*I Am surrounded by Love*

*My Words are powerful it creates a world for me that is Limitless*

*This is your day of YES reclaim your inner peace*

*I declare that I Am Becoming the person that I Am Destined to be.*

***When God's word changes the direction of your***

***life, that change is the turning point to an
extraordinary new beginning.***

*I Am Winning*

*I have an attractive Mindset*

*I will never Lack I just Transition Myself for
Better*

*My Glow is the shining of My Spirit that radiates
at a High frequency, My Fearlessness to be Great,
Strong, Bold and Beautiful*

*I Am Uniquely Me*

*I Walk with my head held high to see the
vision that's in front of me*

*I'm classy woman with Distinction*

*My Presence is Powerful*

*My Words creates as atmosphere of Purpose
and Intentionality*

*My Very existence is a magnetic energy that attracts an abundant life*

*I Am Destined for Greatness*

*I Am the Artist of my life*

*I Am a Peculiar being transmuting and embracing the mindset of abundance*

*My Unique higher self is transforming a life that is divine*

*Self- Expression gives birth to a new reality for both My Soul and*

*Spiritual evolution to the next level*

*The Warrior inside me is Resilient, Brave Determined fueled by the Faith that drives Me*

*The Pureness of My intentions attract a Love that is Effortless*

**The Beauty of my Spirit**
**Shines with Grace**
**My Spirit is Powerful and**
**Inviting**

*It transcends Positive*
*Vibrations*
*The Warmth of the vibrant colors*
*Allures you to Grow*
*I AM who I AM because of the*
*Spirit Within My Spirit is like*
*the Sun it brings PEACE*
                              *- R. Davis*

*I'm a Boss in my world*

*Rise UP, Rise Up know that you are Worthy*

*My Unwavering Fiery Spirit bring forth the*
*manifestation to the fruition of the words I Speak*
*over my life*

*I Am Worthy of all things that I desire*

*I Know that I AM Enough*

*I Will Embrace myself in every season*

*I Am Walking in Authority*

*I Am vibrating at a High Frequency*

*I Am everything I want to Be*

*I AM Blessed*

*I Am an Overcomer*

*I Am a Conquer*

*I Am Unstoppable because I Am always Elevating*

*I Am Gifted*

*I AM a Whole Vibe*

*I Am Confident*

*Greatness exudes from Me*

*I Am Bold and Beautiful*

*My Hands, Head and Heart are aligned with my Spirit*

*I Am Happiness*

*I Am a Righteous Child of the Most High*

*I Am the Chief Architect of My Life*

*I Am Victorious*

**Do You Not Know and Understand that you are the Temple of God, and that the Spirit of God Dwells in YOU: 1 Cor 3:16**
**(AMP)**

*I have a Winning Spirit*

*I Am walking in Victory*

*I Am Light*

*My Faith moves Mountains*

*I AM Kind*

*I Am Love*

*I Am Fearless*

*I Am a Shining Star*

*I Choose Me*

*I Am a Creative Soul*

*I Am Fierce*

*I Am Resilient*

*I can be What I want*

*I Value the gift that I was given*

*I Choose to Celebrate Me*

*I Choose to be Present*

*I Am Royalty*

*I Am Grateful*

*I Am a Warrior*

*I Am a Reaper of my Harvest*

*I Walk by Faith not by Sight*

*My Spirit is Awakened*

*I Am Beautiful*

*I Am Fearfully and Wonderfully made*

*I Am Thriving*

**The Secret of Change is to focus all your energy not on fighting the old, but on building the new**

**-Socrates**

*I Am Courageous*

*I Am Pure Energy*

*I Am Deserving*

*My growth is Limitless*

*I Am a Reflection of my Strength*

*I Believe in Myself*

*I Choose to be Proud of Who I AM*

*I Choose to have Inner Peace*

*I Am Peace*

*I Am Unapologetically Free and Embracing a New Me*

*I Am Valuable*

*I have Purpose and Power*

*I Am fearless in the face of Others*

*I Am Deeply Rooted within Myself*

*I Am a Masterpiece*

*I Am Successful*

*I Am grounded in Gratitude*

*I Am lifted by the Grace of God*

*I Stand in My Power*

*I LOVE Myself*

*I have Wings of an Eagle I Learned to Soar*

*I am a Creative Visionary*

*I Am a Blessed and Educated Queen*

**So shall my words be that goeth forth out of my mouth; it shall not return unto me void, but it shall accomplish that which I please and it shall prosper in the thing where to I sent it.**

*I want to close with this: nothing is impossible to a person who believes in the power that one carries inside of themselves. Love who you are. Accept who you are and believe in the Power of change. Embrace your difference, the unique talents that were given only to you so shine for all the world to see. When you start to minister to your heart an inward experience of peace will start to fester which will then start an outward expression of unconditional love to the world around you. Because you have given yourself permission in the ability to heal from your brokenness by understanding that you are the key element which is love of self. Through the transformation of your mindset to have a renewed insight of what you want it to look like. Being more confident in your skin and having the character to follow. Having Faith and knowing that He is always with you.*

## Sun Goddess

*I Bling, Like a Shining Star that Glows all over the World.*

*My Spirit is as Sweet and Vibrant as a Bouquet of Earths'*

## Prettiest Flowers

*When I Speak It's Sound of Thunder because I Speak to My*

## Circumstances

*I Dictate my Future by Calling it into Existence*
*When I move, The Earth Calibrates On its Axis to Adjust to my Power*
*So when You See a Goddess Steppin' N Struttin, Smile and Say....*
*Glow Girl Glow!!!*
*Like, The Rising Sun SHINE!!!*

*- Anonymous*

*I am the daughter of a King who is not moved by the world for my God is with me and goes before me. I don't fear because I AM HIS.*